Disney's
Winnie the Pooh
Try, Try Again

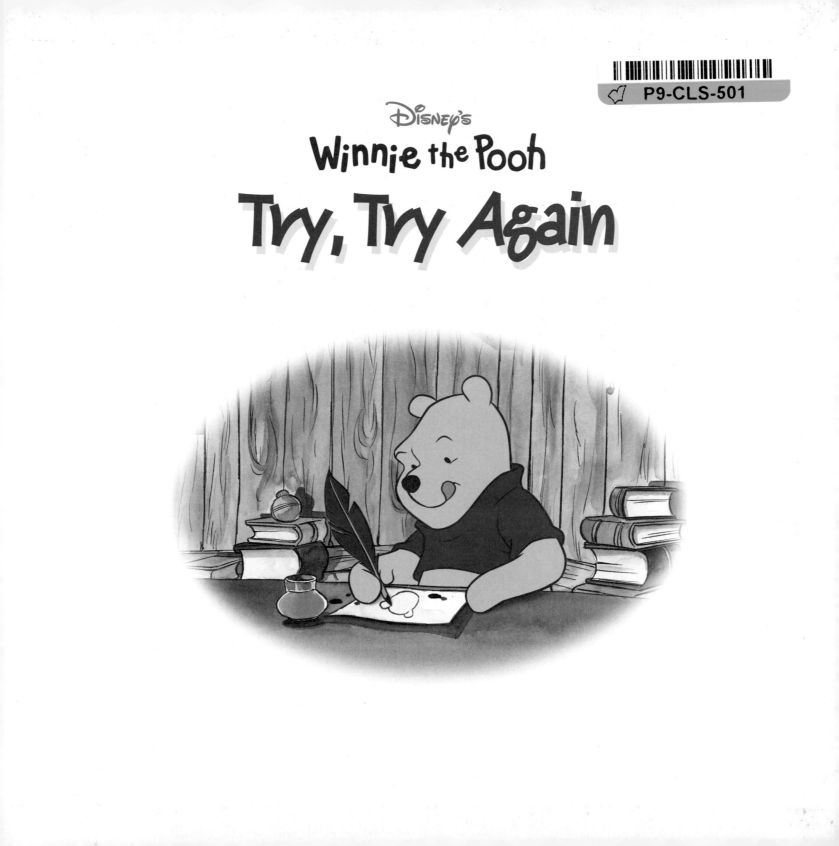

Learning to write

Can take some time—

Like counting up to ten.

But you'll be writing

Just like Pooh,

If you try, try again.

Poor Pooh was at home recovering from the sniffles.
When he woke up from a nap, he saw a little note under his door.
It looked like a get-well card signed: "Love, Christopher Robin."

"I wonder if I could write my name," Pooh thought.
And since he was feeling much better, Pooh sat down at his
table with paper and pencils.

Pooh tried his best, but he wasn't quite sure if he'd gotten it right.
"If only I knew how to write my name," he sighed.
Suddenly Pooh had an idea.

Pooh ran over to one of his honey pots. "Maybe honey will work better than a pencil," he thought.

Pooh dipped his hand in the honey. But try as he might to write a "P," it didn't work. All he had was a sticky mess on paper.

Pooh stopped to lick the paper clean. Honey made a tasty bit of writing—too bad no one could read it!

"Rabbit and Owl are very smart," thought Pooh. "Perhaps they could teach me how to write my name."

Pooh went straight to Rabbit's house.

"You can use these to write your name," Rabbit suggested, pointing to the carrots and tomatoes.

Pooh gave it a try, but all he saw were vegetables everywhere.

Pooh looked down at the carrots and tomatoes. "Have you any honey?" he asked.

Rabbit knew that their lesson was over.

"Come back tomorrow," he insisted. "We'll try again."

After stopping at home for a smackerel of honey, Pooh went over to Owl's house.

Owl assured him that learning to write his name would be no problem at all. He simply needed a good writing instrument.

Owl went to his desk and pulled out a beautiful feather pen.
Then he took out a piece of paper and a little jar of ink. He
dipped the pen in the ink and wrote "Phoo."

"Now you try," Owl said, handing Pooh the pen.

Pooh took the pen and looked down at the paper. He took a
deep breath and began to write.

"Oh, bother," said Pooh. "Does this look right to you?"

Pooh had drawn a picture of himself.

"Ah," said Owl. "You just need a little more practice. Why don't you come back tomorrow?"

Pooh nodded. All this trying had made him very tired.

On his way home, Pooh met Tigger. He told Tigger that he wanted to learn how to write his name.

"I got just the thing, Buddy Bear!" Tigger cried. "See ya soon!"

Pooh no sooner got home, had a snack, and was about to lie down, when Tigger bounced through his door. He brought Christopher Robin's wagon full of paints and paintbrushes.

Tigger told Pooh that since he was having trouble writing his name, maybe he could paint it! Painting was a lot more fun than writing!

"Oh, dear," said Pooh. "Perhaps I could give it a try."
But before Pooh had a chance to begin, Tigger got
busy painting.

Before long, Tigger got bored and bounced off into the Wood.
"TTFN! Ta-Ta For Now!" Tigger called, bouncing away.
 Poor Pooh was more confused than before!
Now he would never learn how to write his name!

The very next day, Pooh and Piglet made plans to meet each other. When Pooh arrived, Piglet decided to visit Christopher Robin to ask for his help.

Soon Christopher Robin walked up to Pooh carrying a large writing pad. "Hello, Pooh," he said with a smile.

"Why, hello, Christopher Robin," Pooh said. "I'm waiting for Piglet. He's going to help me learn to write my name."

"Piglet just told me. Maybe I can help, too," said Christopher Robin.

Writing just one letter at a time, Christopher Robin showed Pooh how to do it.

"Now you try, Pooh," Christopher Robin said. Then he had Pooh copy each letter. Pooh wrote very slowly. *P-O-O-H.*

Piglet came by and saw that Pooh had written his name.
"Look, Piglet!" Pooh cried.
"We just have to work on the *P*," laughed Christopher Robin.
"It's backwards."

"Oh, Pooh!" Piglet cried. "You've done it. You wrote your name just as you said you would. You just had to keep trying."

"Well," said Pooh, "all that trying wasn't easy, but it was worth it! Now there's one more word I'd like to write!"

"Go ahead," Christopher Robin said. So Pooh gave it his best try. "H-U-N-Y," Pooh wrote slowly, licking his lips.

"Silly old bear," laughed Christopher Robin. "Let me show you." He took the pencil and wrote: "Pooh loves honey!"

The next morning when Piglet got out of bed, he saw a little white envelope under his door. He couldn't wait to open it.

Piglet read the note aloud. It said: "Pooh loves *Piglet* and *honey*," and it was signed "Pooh."

"Hooray for Pooh!" Piglet shouted as he raced toward his friend's house to congratulate him. Piglet couldn't wait to tell Pooh how proud he was that Pooh had learned to write his name–and that he had done it by try-try-trying his very best.

A LESSON A DAY POOH'S WAY

Instead of just sighing,

Pooh keeps on trying.